Second Acts in

AMERICAN LIVES

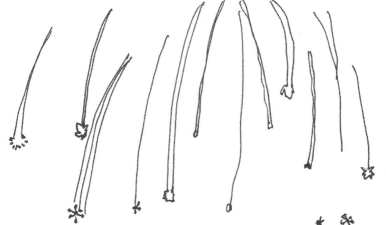

Second Acts in AMERICAN LIVES

~ flash stories ~

RYAN RIDGE

& MEL BOSWORTH

Illustrations by Jacob Heustis

Alternating Current Press
Boulder, Colorado

Second Acts in American Lives
Ryan Ridge & Mel Bosworth
©2018 Alternating Current Press

Alternating Current
Boulder, Colorado
alternatingcurrentarts.com

ISBN-10: 1-946580-03-1
ISBN-13: 978-1-946580-03-0
First Edition: March 2018

To Russell.
And for Fran.

Advance Praise

"Short fiction from two masters of the form."

—*NERVE*

"Ranging from short to super-duper short, the prose-poetic stories in Ryan Ridge's and Mel Bosworth's *Second Acts in American Lives* zig and zag, fake and fade, keeping the reader guessing on every page, and the illustrations by Jacob Heustis are every bit as funny and surprising as the words they accompany. It's a pinball machine of a book, full of bounce and light and crazy ricochets: sentences start, you don't know where they'll end up, and this dynamic unpredictability is what gives this collection its life and its victory."

—Kathleen Rooney,
author of *Lillian Boxfish Takes a Walk*

"A collection of wildly imaginative capsules of surrealist Americana. The short punchy pieces are chaotic enough to be funny and tragic enough to be heartbreaking."

—*Preview Massachusetts Magazine*

"Swallow this book like it's the last cold Michelob Ultra. Read it, do a little dance, then take it out back and shoot it. Take down this book like it's the last thing you will ever do in this life, because I'm telling you, it most likely will be. Be with this book, and I mean be with it. Is it poetry? Is it prose? Who the hell cares. Bosworth and Ridge are great literary beasts by themselves, to be read often and carefully. Together they have become one wild fucking animal. These are the real bits of us, the hidden bits and the exposed, laid out in one stunning sentence after another. I'll always keep *Second Acts in American Lives* close by. I cried laughing. I have never read anything like it."

—Ryan MacDonald,
author of *The Observable Characteristics of Organisms*

"Twenty things I want to say about Mel Bosworth and Ryan Ridge: 1.) Did Poetry write these men into being? 2.) Poetry was in a weird mood. 3.) They're good, you should know. 4.)

Like really, really good. 5.) Repeat winners of Sentence of the Year. 6.) Where do they get off? 7.) Where do they get on, for that matter? 8.) Can they show other writers the place? 9.) Scratch that last question. 10.) What I was meaning to say: there should be laws against these men. 11.) Or at least a temporary injunction. 12.) It's like, Hold on! 13.) We need to catch our breaths! 14.) We need to unpretzel our minds! 15.) Breath nets. 16.) Mind. ... 17.) What? 18.) Look what you've done to me here. 19.) Just look. 20.) See what I mean?"

—Scott Garson,
author of *Is That You, John Wayne?*

"From precocious Buddhas to out-of-control vehicles, Ridge and Bosworth will take you on their own unique, highly experimental but effectual journey. You can't help but enjoy exploring the very short form with these two creative minds and marvel at how they bring out the best in each other."

—Tara Lynn Masih,
Founding Series Editor of *The Best Small Fictions*

"Antic, exuberant, and full of surprise, almost every sentence ends on a note of provocative mystery, pointing toward the pregnant darkness where David Berman disappeared. These brief, jagged stories are punky, druggy, and beautifully poetic. They'll take you on a warp-speed ramble through an America that's died and come back and died again, getting stranger and punchier every time. Why fear the coming apocalypse if it's this much fun?"

—David Leo Rice,
author of *A Room in Dodge City*

TABLE OF CONTENTS

There are no second acts in American lives.
—F. Scott Fitzgerald

Every cigarette tasted "taxed" and the Feds were closing in
on us, the last smokers in Marlboro Country.

When they caught us, out behind Barracuda Bartending School,
they searched the Thunderbird and played Good Addiction /
Bad Addiction with its contents.

Forced to surrender our illicit tobacco,
robbed of our street-legal weed.

We learned to subsist on Salvia, NicotineWater, and PowerBars.

And we got real comfortable living out our creative nonfictions
in places like Canada, Colorado and Juarez, Texas.

Bottom Blood

A pack of biographers chased me into the Hollywood Forever Cemetery. They cornered me at John Huston's grave. One of the men said, "Take his wrists." I let my eyes relax so I could see their hands in a kind of panorama. I suspected they knew karate. They collapsed like sunset shadows on a mountainside, and I felt the hard bite. A boy bulled between their torsos and collected me on a roll of parchment. At 3rd, 4th, 5th grade, I could still make out the red lines. By the time we reached high school, the thinness had moved in, the bottom blood, which meant I had to trust them not to fuck up my senior prom. Pretty Melinda curled beside me in the lime-green Dart as we tore donut after donut on Gill's hayfield, the moon so fat and tired. Yes, that was living. As opposed to this: buried here beneath the weight of my own life story and so much dirt.

Summer Somewhere

A second ago it was September. A second before that we were sitting in my basement on beanbag chairs, listening to the latest Bob Dylan album. Your hair was stringy and wind-blown. My motorcycle helmet was not yet cracked. I put it on. You said, "Dylan faked that motorcycle accident." I flipped up the visor so I could speak and said, "Get out. Tell me more." You said, "There's nothing more to tell. He faked it. It didn't happen." I said, "But why? Why did he fake it?" You said, "He needed a break." I said, "We could all use something like that." You said, "It's always summer somewhere." I said, "Come on. Let's ride until we find it."

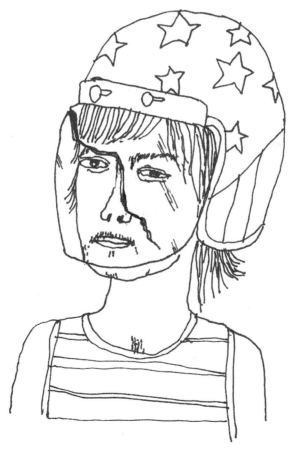

LITTLE BUDDY

Buddy Brando's last words were an advertising slogan. Standing in front of the state firing squad in the lightning and the rain, he spoke between cracks of thunder: "Nothing beats a cold Bud." The bullets unzipped his chest, creating a hole big enough for a smaller Buddy to escape from.

THE POET ADDRESSES
A PROUD NATION

Everywhere: ash, and Christmas lights. "No, you're doing it wrong," you said. I said, "Who the hell knows how to tie a bow tie anymore?" And you leaned in and tied it for me, the trails from your cigarette forming stately wisps around your nostrils. I shook your shaking hand and thanked you. "So this is it," I said. "It's time." You said, "It's always time, and time is always. *Per aspera ad astra.*" I attempted to wrap my mind around it. I failed as usual. You said, "We will go on continuing to continually continue—" but you trailed off as the television cameras rolled. I rolled my eyes as you took the stage in your corduroy suit, cigarette extinguished but not quite out. It was so damn cold that night in the outdoor amphitheater that it looked like you were still smoking after the fact. My heart beatboxed badly as you leaned into the microphone and said, "My fellow countrymen and women, I regret to inform you that I don't have enough middle fingers for you all." And later, after your speech, when they shot us in our throats, I saw stars. Stars everywhere. Stars falling everywhere and on everyone. Everyone was a star and nothing is real.

Where the Doors Went

Papa was a Stones fan. The John McEnroe of table tennis. A total remote-control freak. He slept with the television on and went off about tax cuts. If there wasn't anything to fix, he'd break shit. My first car, for instance. Back in '86. *Top Gun* was rocking the box office. I was rocking my lime-green Dart. Pops was rocking a sixer of Schlitz and running his mouth about how he wanted to "learn me about cars." Two weeks later the old man had rebuilt much of the engine with junkyard parts and high-temp epoxy. Two weeks after that, he was dead. Clay pigeon. We never did figure out where the doors went. We never did figure out how he drove that Dart clean across the river only to crash it into an oak on the other side. At the time, I was too scared to open my eyes. At the time, I believed in love and I reckon I still do.

ESCAPE TO NO ESCAPE

Using the cherry of my cigarette, I set all the fuses to sizzling. Then I ran-scrambled over the fence, dove through the hedge, and somersaulted and somersaulted and somersaulted and somersaulted before finally tumbling to a rocking stop beside you. You said, "Kid, I don't think it caught, which is good considering you left a trail of gasoline leading right to us." It was true. Then the explosion, and we tried to run but it was a short run. Your last words? Unintelligible. My last words? *My bad.*

Swapping Spit

At the cemetery with the wittiest epitaphs. Witnessing headstones shot by
Leicas. My mohawk made me feel clos-
er to God despite my atheism. My hands
molded your face, and we kissed hard.
My eyes were closed when the boy with
the bloodied scroll tripped past us. Your
eyes were closed when the man with the
bloodied arms was dragged past us. Our
tongues curled and snapped, swapped
secrets, spit.

Salad Days

She was late to the party. I stayed home. I imagined wild animals. I filled every bowl in the house with salad she'd bought and waited for the neighborhood kids to come. It was Halloween. I'd been doing my best to cultivate a plant persona. I had more bongs than friends. When the doorbell rang, I asked the little vampires if they wanted Italian or Ranch. They went with Ranch. I went to bed early because it was never too late to turn things around. Tomorrow, I thought, is the first day of the rest of my gym membership.

I Said What I Said

You said, "Remind me to remind you."
And I said, "I said what I said." This
was all before the bumpy carriage ride
and after the thing with the hearse.
Three streets, remember? We were three
sheets to the wind. You were still wearing makeup then. I was still wearing my
heart on my cardigan. Later, beneath a
sagging hemlock, you said, "Panther,"
and I said a word neither of us believed.

Midnight Safari

They craned their necks to look at the hard parts of the sky. The meteor shower was supposed to be at its best and brightest that night. They were giraffes. From the brush, we admired them through our rifle sites. Kitty said to shoot, but my trigger finger wouldn't pull. Above us, meteors swirled. The sky looked like a drain. Kitty said, "I'm more of a man than you." And I did not disagree, because it was true. Truer still was her aim.

The Next Hieroglyph

I'd been biding time in a roofless gazebo. I watched the clouds pass like backup point guards. Tall guy for a layup. Fat guy for a missed dunk. It didn't matter and the clouds didn't mind, and I didn't mind, either, having no mind to mind. It was like childhood that way, a plastic shovel moving sand in a sandbox. Though sooner than later I'd have to leave this gazebo, this forest, push on, find the next bank, the next hieroglyph. At first the Egyptians were hot in the biscuit, but I'd cooled them off like apple pies on windowsills. Now, staring at icicles forming on clouds —drops of breast milk slipping off nipples —I can nearly hear the chickens coming home to roost. And farther off still, I can nearly hear the low rumble of something bigger than you on your loudest day.

The Biggest Hearts in the World Cannot Be Tethered

Ignition coil purchased. Tomorrow
we install it. This rocket has moons
to love.

Beneath the rainforest, there is a city.

In the sky

a wounded moon.

BIG RAIN

The nightly news ended on an ominous note. A woman whipped up a batch of blueberry pancakes in the kitchenette of their tiny home. In the adjoining room, her husband took off his boots after a long day of looking for work from the foldout couch. These are people who make do. They get by. They'll weather whatever. They've eaten breakfast for dinner for years with a smile. Outside the rain fell like empires.

Sitcom Stars
Storm the Beach

At nightfall, we ran aground. Faint stars and fainter tails of comets like bullwhips. Passengers fainting face-first onto the sand. I thought, turn them like this. Good. Make it more like the movies. We eureka'ed the MDMA powder with vacuum-like precision, and soon enough our hands joined like people who join cults joined—we were joiners—and afterward we said a little prayer that tonight would outshine the notion of night and that we would survive to tell the tale to some fat network execs and maybe even add a scene or two in our inevitable biopics. Now the fainters were up and the bonfire was lit, and just as the orgy was about to shift into the next gear, we heard the sound of the sky slicing then gulls crying, and then we watched a helicopter white-knuckle it onto the beach. Out of the black bird popped a famous film director renowned for wearing dual eye patches when he directs. Good. We are actors, dammit, children who never ceased believing. Give us direction.

Return to Rikers

At the second-run movie theater where you get the two-for-one on popcorn tubs and a one-eyed projectionist nurses warm beer between changeovers, we ceded our coins to the dwarf at the concession stand. When the theater darkened, we permitted our minds to dream in public. They were showing the sequel to a prison-break film called *Return to Rikers*. All of the actors were C-list, but we didn't care. We had fantastic mohawks and the world by the balls.

Our Tolerance of Youth

We heard Kmart country leaking from a rusted El Dorado. Then we heard there was no truth in politics. Still, we pursued happiness, which for us meant selling medicinal marijuana scripts in order to supplement our true passion: lawn darts. We plunged ChemLawns and natural lawns and golf courses up and down the West Coast until the money ran out. Then we got ripped and ran into ourselves, explored the inner workings of our daydreams until night fell, and so did your mother. We stayed the winter in the Rockies, slept in separate beds, and encouraged Mom's brittle hip to mend using myriad herbal remedies and quasi-urban shamanism. We watched gobs of MTV, wondered whatever happened to our tolerance of youth, the cast of the first *Real World*, good music. During commercials we drew pictures of each other and pressed them against the picture window in the living room. I made your hair blue and your mother's hair red. You'd never heard the deep belly laugh of a mountain before. I'd never known simple pleasures so easy.

Tonight I Will Use My One Phone Call from Jail to Ask You to Marry Me

Outside the bagel shop, the police mistook my sign language for gang signs. I was focused on your lips, how your mouth moved, vibrations. Good vibrations. I took a knee. Through the giant bagel marquee, I watched the sunset burst from the center and thought how everything good comes from the center. I was feeling centered. I was feeling good. In fact, I was just about to pop the question when the pigs swarmed. It wasn't so good what those cops did to me. But you are something else. Yes, you are. And I have only one question for you now ...

FREELANCERS

She opened her laptop and closed it and opened it again. I unlocked my phone and checked my email. Nothing. I turned on the flat-screen and changed the channel and changed the channel and changed the channel. I said, "I can do this all day." She said, "Maybe this freelancing isn't working out so well." I turned off the TV and said, "Maybe you're right. How many years of school will I need in order to get back into school?" She said, "Too many." And I didn't even have to say that I'd already had enough. She knew. I said, "I quit." She said, "You can't *quit* freelancing." I said, "Watch me." And then I didn't move. For a very long time, I did not move. The office phone rang. "You're going to answer it," she said. I said, "Hello ..." I said, "Interesting." I said, "I don't know." I said, "Let me see what she says." I hung up. "Who was that?" she said. "Your father," I said. "And?" she said. "And he offered us a job," I said. "Yay," she said. "What's the job?" "Well," I said, "he needs help writing your stepmother's obituary." "But my stepmother isn't dead," she said. "That's the thing," I said. "That's where we come in."

A String of Hot Seconds

The stars glittered like strippers' chests, and you said, "I give you my word." I said, "Not so fast! How about we just start with a letter?" My uncle always warned me a promise is only as good as the person who says it. You were as good as gone: I'd found your bus ticket to Mexico. You hit the jets and the bubbles bubbled up between my legs. My genitals danced. Some hard minutes passed until finally we softened them with the spit in our cheeks. Through the gap in your front teeth you hissed a string of hot seconds that swirled in the whirlpool between us. Despite your secrets there was something in your face that told me I should take a chance. When I turned around to put on some Van Halen, you jammed a steak knife between my shoulder blades and I slipped beneath the water for the big sleep. You cranked the tub up to boiling, and my dying mind got fixed on a loop of my uncle throwing down his cowboy hat outside a saloon. Through the dust that kicked up all around, my eyes kept returning to the horses tethered near-by, their long faces blank and beautiful as catwalk amnesiacs.

Paradise City Forever

Using broken furniture and a nail gun, the man reinforced the doors and windows. The woman explained to the remaining children that the Easter Bunny was sick in the head. Using duct tape and recycled materials from the broken doors and windows, the man set to work erecting a crude chair right there in the living room. The woman explained to the remaining children that the seat would serve as the terrestrial throne for the coming Messiah. Their eldest son, Little Bobby, was an eighteen-year-old who never went through puberty. He suffered from a rare disease known as Little Bobby's Disease—where the patient remains trapped in a twelve-year-old's body and has trouble remembering reasons to get excited about the world. Once the man put the finishing touches on the throne, he stepped back to admire his handiwork, and that's when Little Bobby sat down wearing a loincloth and refused to get up. He crossed his legs and said, "And so it begins. I have come here to judge the living and the dead. Let's start with you, Pops. If this throne is any indication of your carpentry skills, then I'll say this: thank God you aren't an electrician. And Mom, I hate to tell you this, but you're adopted. Sorry. Your real family is next door. Go, be with them. And finally the good news: the rest of you bastards will be with me in Paradise City forever. Let us now drink from the bottled water of eternal life."

No One Can Hear the Cotton Screams of Ronnie James Dio

Years later we were like a worm separated by a bicycle wheel: inaugurating our end during closing time at a restaurant marred by salad bars. Playing footsie with future dividends. Toasting each other posthumously. Turning off our wedding rings forever. There we were in our minds, skin naked and pink, teeth-tearing our favorite concert tees and slam-dancing with mechanics, each of us happier and each of us the wiser for it.

It All Almost

A dog on the grass, chewing on a toy: as stupid and beautiful as anything I've ever seen. And I've seen it all almost.

Exaltation

It was a super-secret surprise party one second, and the next? Authorities showed up hardly looking like authorities. Still we left. It was Christmas Eve in Pensacola, and she said the dog track was our best bet. We sat on the bleachers watching the night sky explode white and pink. I said, "Santa's in trouble." You rubbed your belly and said, "This baby isn't yours." Later beneath the saltwater sun, bullet dogs race-ripped the track as I shuffled westward toward the next best-kept.

Runaway Rex

They took my keys. I took their money. I slipped across the border where cartel wars raged. I chose a side. I joined the fight. I took many scalps. We all won. We all lost. We all learned something we'd forget then remember again. You once told me you can't stomach children. I still can't believe in dogs that come home.

When *The Battle of Algiers* ejected from the VCR,
we felt like rival gangs shot by the same documentarian.

As Jack from "Jack and the Beanstalk"
resurfaced in a Hazard County yarn.

We saw hummingbirds nesting in paradoxical chevrons.

Out where acid rain falls on Empire Condominiums

and sad clusters of offices are referred to as parks.

Q: What the hell kind of park forces petite women
to wear massive shoulder pads?

TUXEDO DOGS

Weekends, Dad liked to pick up drifters and drop them off in inconvenient places for fun. I think this had something to do with the fact his own father ran a fat camp for obese canines out by the county line. Mom thought it had something to do with sex, like some weird sex thing. I just thought it was that maybe he preferred the company of strangers. Maybe it was the smell of their skin or forced small talk that attracted him? I think that, mostly. The company thing, not so much the smell thing. And I think of those obese canines dressed in black tuxedos, shirts, unwashed corduroys, planets.

LOST SCENES FROM THE LITTLE LEAGUE WORLD SERIES PARKING LOT

A man yelling for us to put it down. "Put that down right now!" The sun in our eyes, then the moon. Then two moons. Then more men and more things to put down. A banjo-playing lunatic. A grieving mother. A helpless guru. Softballs the size of cantaloupes. The sense of cinematic finality every time we stubbed our cigarettes into beer cans. Then more cans. Bottles. Then two suns. Then two nuns and more things to put down like our habits. We kicked our heroin spoons across the parking lot and fell down in front of a Winnebago, muttering nonsense. Then live music: Deadheads on mandolins. Then birds flying upside down like jokes. Luchadores fighting at the taco truck. Women in sexy pioneer costumes crossing their fingers. Men in Black Sabbath tees. A man yelling, "Aspirin, Disneyland!" Another man dousing himself in kerosene as his wife bursts into laughter from the flames. At least that's how I remember it.

Separated at Birth

I was numb from beer when I saw my ex-wife's name graffitied on the side of a bank. It was Christmas morning. Pigeons decamped from the roof of the bank to the roof of another bank. Another man numb on beer stood looking at his ex-wife's name graffitied on the side of the other bank. We took simultaneous sips of beer and flashed on the long-lost brother we never had. On Christmas, my father always gave me a carton of Lucky Strikes. The other man's father always gave him another piece of a deconstructed lawn-mower and a check that would bounce.

Everything's True Intention

Later, in a bookstore called Read 'em & Weep, we heard a lone voice shouting from the American Lit section. It said, "Don't count on frontier sermons getting you laid, pilgrims!" I froze. You froze, too, two seconds later. A dog that had followed us froze with a copy of *War and Peace* in its mouth. Time and space rippled like a Jolly Roger in the wind. Then everything else froze. Outside, streetlights popped like popcorn. Tiny bits of glass gathered like snow on the head and shoulders of a frozen farmer who was sitting on a frozen bench in a frozen park with a frozen pond. The man's arm was outstretched to give a frozen piece of bread to a frozen swan, though it could have been the other way around. One end of the bread was in the man's hand and the other end was in the swan's beak, so it was hard to tell exactly where one ended and the next began. Much later, everything's true intention was revealed when the sun split our skin and bookmarked our bleeding hearts.

The House Always Wins

The only thing I've learned in life is never second-guess your second choices. I imparted this wisdom to the boys at the kitchen table. "Did you hear that, Will? I mean—Tom? Did you hear that, kids?" I stood swiveling back and forth between children, finger pointing fake pistols. The pressure was getting to me. I needed guts. I needed conviction. I needed a dark beer, a real beard, and a semi-automatic weapon. The boys needed to finish their oatmeal and go to school. Then someone tossed a brick through the kitchen window, and I jumped so high I almost glimpsed God's sandals. The brick was wrapped in a note that read: *YOU WILL DIE A HAPPY DEATH*. I'd seen enough. I re-wrapped the brick and tossed it back out the window. "There are such awful people out there," I told the boys as I wiped their tears and combed their hair. "There are such awful and wonderful things in this world we should never see." I brushed their eyes closed with my fingertips, cocooned them in a gauze of camouflage, and strapped them to my legs. I said, "You comfortable?" My left leg/Will: "Yeah." My right leg/Tom: "What? Yeah." Then I strapped every pellet gun I had to my vest. It was time to see the world again. It was time to face the music. It was time to show my bookie that this time I was holding a full house of love.

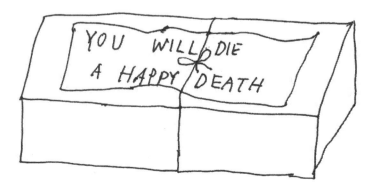

Cuckolding down the Fort

After dinner, we made cribs of oak. The act made you smaller, and you showed surprising dexterity that belied your tree-like girth. Back east, a cold front had moved into your old bedroom. In your old living room, your husband walked through the door, removed his hat, and wiped his brow. In your old life, he was cast as a villain, but I am so much worse than that now.

Our Flag Was Still There

She said we'll have to buy tickets to the
Jack & Jill, but we'll get free food and
drinks. She said it's in October. I put on
my comfortable nighttime pants. It was
midafternoon. July 5th. A Sunday. I was
still drunk from the day before. She said
we'll have to fly, but we'll get SkyMiles.
She said it's in Detroit, and she said a lot
of other things, too, but by then I'd
stopped listening. Outside, I heard either
gunshots or fireworks, but I decided it was
gunshots. Definitely gunshots. "Quick," I
said. "Hand me a beer!" She slid me a
case of warm PBR, and I fell in love with
my country all over again.

YOUR LIFE AND NEARLY MINE

Your itinerant father called to extol the virtues of childlessness. On television, they flashed a sketch of the Salt Water Taffy Strangler. It looked an awful lot like your ex-yoga-instructor lover. I smeared camouflage across my cheeks, signaled for you to pass me the bong: two fingers up, rabbit ears, then down, up, down, up, just like we'd practiced. You pinched your cell phone between your ear and shoulder, rubbed the underside of your baby bump with one hand, signaled for me to wait with the other: hard fist, unmoving. I repeated the bong signal but added a slashing motion across my throat, which meant, "Hurry up." You mistook it as a confession that I was the S. W. T. Strangler. My signal also could've meant "cut the call," and I failed to explain this to you between shotgun blasts that tore holes in the walls and the furniture and chased me from your life and nearly mine. That was twelve years ago. These days I'm a seasoned seasonal rider of freight trains, zipping and unzipping the states as I hope to find the real S. W. T. Strangler. Speaking of, I'm slow-hoping for a re-union/reconciliation. I can't hear my son's voice, and that's something I really want to hear. Hell, I miss you, too. And when the day finally comes, the reunion signal will be easy because I practice it all the time inside the saddest boxcar: knees to chest, hug forever.

THE TIME I GOT INTO A KNIFE FIGHT BUT FORGOT MY KNIFE

The rain came down like daggers. You wore a weird expression and worried that your skirt made you look like a whore. I worried about death. On this street: men with weapons all around us. I said, "Let's walk a little faster, shall we?" You said, "But these heels. I can't walk fast in these heels." I said, "I thought whores were always fast." I was kidding, but you weren't laughing.

MEMPHIS BLOOD

As I was falling out, the doctor said, "Damn, this birth is loud!" And I heard an orderly say, "Wow!" My mother sucked a hard breath and held it like a straightjacket. My father's right foot stalled over the drum pedal as the awestruck orderly toweled me off. Daylight punched my eyes and my eyes punched back and then someone slipped a drumstick into my hand. "Jam!" my mother screeched. "Jam! Jam! Jam!" My father nudged the splash cymbal toward the gurney, and my mother stuffed my mouth with her left nipple. My lips tightened around the flesh, and my fingers tightened around the oak. My father's right foot crushed the drum pedal, and the bass exploded like Civil War cannon. Between deep belts and howls, my mother dazzled the reeds of her blues harp with her tongue. The groove wrapped the room like a second skin, and my Memphis blood took us all home.

ELVIS COSTELLO HAS LEFT THE BUILDING

The opening band closed. We set
our hair on fire.

Tꜱe Events
ᴀs Tꜱey Unfolded

They found the car stripped in the desert.
They found you stripping in a dive just
outside Tucson. They told me you looked
as good as ever. They told me I could
come along, but I'd have to hang back
with Hector. Hector was their technician.
I'd get to see it all go down on a tiny
monitor. But the monitor in question
turned out to offer an unexceptional view.
In fact, it offered no view at all, as it was
an analog baby monitor. According to
Hector, however, if I closed my eyes and
listened, I'd have a play-by-play of the
events as they unfolded. The problem was
when I closed my eyes, all I heard was
monitor static and tires. And when I
opened my eyes, all I saw was taillights
canceled by the six o'clock sun.

IV.

A man who runs a convenience store
sells the convenience store

and then buys another convenience store
many miles from the original convenience store

when his wife leaves him.

An Introduction to
Gender and Sexuality

Dad drove to a campground and said, "Welcome to college!" He pointed to a stand of oaks beyond the municipal showers and said, "Future books." Then he pointed to me and said, "Future grad." Then he pointed to himself and said, "Future woman." Then he pointed to the cooler and said, "Let's have a final manly beer!" Later, pensive and buzzed beside the crackle of our campfire, I took a cool swallow of Michelob Ultra, fired a snot rocket into the darkness, and told my father he'd make a damn fine mother.

GO WILDCATS!

He decided to propose during inter-
course. Here's what he proposed:
"How about I take this condom off?"
She accepted, then presented a propo-
sition of her own: "How about we run
off together and save this tired old
world from itself?" His eyes moved
from her bare breast implants to the
dimple on her chin to the picture of her
parents with her little brother on the
nightstand and hey, her mother is still
hot, which is a good sign, and then his
eyes hardened with purpose on her
eyes and his lips parted and he was
about to answer when suddenly her
little brother tripped from her closet
wearing her old cheerleader uniform.
"Go Wildcats!" the boy shouted. "Go,
Fight, Win! Go, Fight, Win!" Everybody won that night, but the following
morning war machines crowded the
earth, sea, and sky. Nine months later
the post-apocalyptic world had its
budding savior, and the Wildcats had
their brightest prospect since never.

BEST WESTERN

Then it was the sequel to civilization and our credit cards didn't work anymore and manners didn't matter: all the hotel rent-a-cops were acting rude in the parking lot, cursing and lying and trying to lure our prostitutes away from us with their love batons—scene missing. Later, after the shootout with the sheriff and his heavy friends ended, we agreed on two things, my partner Kitty and I: (1) We felt cool in handcuffs, and (2) the only frontier left was in our minds—our dirty, filthy minds, which would soon be washed.

Different Jurisdictions

We searched the creek for your old man. You said you loved him. I splashed cool water onto my sunburned arms and pretended I did, too. We walked the trails that trailed off like idiots, and I considered the way your father considered me. And sure, he was probably right by his estimates considering I was the CEO of an unsuccessful ayahuasca travel agency and he was an old-school son of a bitch who ran the grand jury, but even so his good judgment couldn't keep him from himself. When they finally found him hanging from his tie in a Broward County brothel closet, I couldn't help but close my eyes and pray that the judges of the next world didn't bring their gavels down as quickly as he did.

I Read the News Today

Convinced my parole officer was a Peeping Tom, I did what any concerned citizen (who just so happens to be an ex-middleman on house arrest) would do: I traded the last of my stash to my neighbor for a pair of night-vision goggles and a crossbow pistol. The plan was to camp out on the screened-in porch and catch the freak in the act. And that night, catch him in the act, I did. The only problem was he caught me, too, and first. Our respective night-vision goggles nearly kissed through the screen, and, just before the flash, I saw his mouth all big and bent and wicked. The bullet burned a hole through my heart and buried itself in my spine. I got off a shot of my own, though, and, at close range, an arrow fired from a crossbow pistol acts less like an arrow and more like an impact hammer. My P.O. died on my lawn, alone, his nose pressed into a patch of buttercups. Death found me flat on my back on the porch. At least that's what the newspaper said, and I believe them.

Honolulu of the Heart

Inside my Subaru we warmed our hands over the vents. I needed to get the newspaper. You needed not to be alone. The sky was big dawn and yawning winter. "How long?" you asked, and I pushed out my bottom lip. "Not sure. Ten years?" You sat back, fingers flexing, said, "I guess I can live with that." I nodded knowingly and ripped a hidden machete from under my seat. I twisted the blade in front of your face and said, "It's better than dying with this." You: "You're amazing." Me: "I'm never taking you to Hawaii."

Heartbreak Special

She said she'd sell him the bike for fifty bucks. Over a bowl of cold clam chowder, I told her she could get at least a hundred for it on Craigslist. She told me she was giving him the "Heartbreak Special." I said, "That's mighty saintly of you and, given the media-saturated hyper-reality we find ourselves faced with today, saints are rare specimens, indeed. Martyrs happen all the time, but a modern saint is about as rare as a one-armed gymnast." I finished my soup and there was a beat of silence and then she said, "You're right. I'll give him the bike for free."

A Spike in Teen Pregnancy

A clown at the county fair accused my wife of animal hus-
bandry. I said it's a good thing I never know what to do or say
or I'd do or say something right now. It was sunset. You said,
"C'mon." We rolled up our lives like sleeping bags and headed
toward brighter colors and louder music. Then we stood
beneath the Ferris wheel with our arms outstretched, hoping to
gather whatever unwanted lumps tumbled from the baskets.
We agreed to work together. We agreed to stop at a smiling
baby.

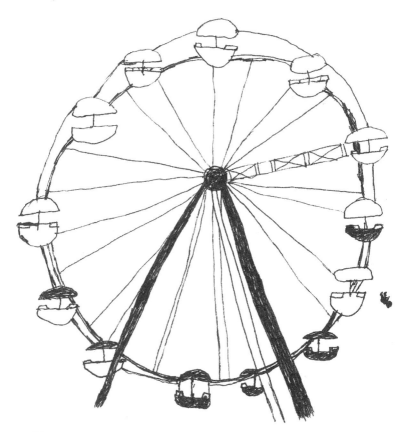

Slick MF

I didn't believe in monsters until my sister brought one home. She called it "Rick." Mom called it "Son!" I called in sick to work for a week and then a month. Ever since Dad died in a golf-cart accident, my life had been punctuated by periods of desperation and despair, and Rick's rapid and pernicious presence (his dog-food franchise, slicked-back hair, and alcoholic eyes) had precipitated in me a new era of agoraphobia. For months I sat in the living room, hardly living on takeout and canned goods (and believe me, there isn't anything good about canned goods). I maxed out my credit and bottomed out on meds. Then it was Easter, and Dad returned from the dead. "Son," he said. "Favor." He asked me to take him to the country club. There was something he'd been meaning to finish. Outside the pro shop, we ran into my sister who confessed, tearfully, that our mother had run away with Rick. Dad tensed up and sis passed out. "Who the hell is Rick?" Dad asked. "Rick," I said, "is just some slick motherfucker."

Donner Party Time

His femur snapped between the rocks, making his legs go nowhere. It was a sound only our stomachs recognized. We were hungry, damned hungry. We licked our lips and lit a fire.

LOVE AND ROPES

I'm breaking your favorite toy when
you stumble into the room. You have
a sandwich in your hand and jelly on
your cheek. You say, "Hey, cut the
shit." And I say, "Hell, no." There is a
small silence we fill with foolish eyes,
and then you kick me in the face. I fall
back onto a toy castle. Stunned, I start
to drown in the moat. You save me
with love and ropes. Later, over a too-
strong hot toddy, I thank you and
apologize for disrespecting not only
our brotherly bond but also the plastic
likeness of Galileo. You accept, but
watch me at odd angles over the next
several years. The oddest angle is from
the planetarium above your bedroom.
I've always meant to ask how you did
that when surrounded by so much
heaven.

LIFE

The medicine stopped working. I put
up new wallpaper, talked to strangers,
tried on different hats.

The rain tumbled along with the Dow.

We saw twin helicopters through toy binoculars.

       Heard: loaded dice and distant thunder.

News Flash: car crash at the intersection of Daycare & Night School.

The rain tumbled along with the Tao.

       Distant dice / loaded thunder.

Like a ticket to nowhere ripped in half:

We were far from one.
It was far from over.

Later, as we were lured into a lurid night club,
       we heard demonic harmonicas blown by the sea.

The Only Way Out Is In

High above, an unnoticed, unmanned drone droned across the blue. Two lovers purred into each other beneath the shell of a school bus. A mangled Missing Person poster flapped in the wind. The wind was thin and sharp and the gutters were marathons of blood and drug-test results. The sewers were in deep shit, too. It was Monday afternoon in the heart of heart-attack country. Most folks were sleeping in if they were smart, and if they were outside they were insane because out here were riot cops and cop-show hosts. Save for those two lovers sucking each other off and on in the street. This street was a dead-end street, a cul-de-sac. There was no way out, and they knew it. They were surrounded. And so they persisted, which, from the drone's HD camera live-feed, looked a lot like love.

It's Alright, Ma
(I'm Only Burning)

My mother sent me a picture of a bird. Along with the picture of the bird was a note that read: *Tell me what kind of bird this is.* I texted: *I don't know, Ma.* You were behind me on the bed. The room felt hot. Hotter than hot. Insanely warm. I could hear your bare legs sliding around beneath the sheets and wondered what you were doing beneath the sheets in this type of heat. Then I heard a series of shrill sounds followed by a loud squawk, and when I turned around, you had turned into a bright purple bird. I took a picture of you on my phone, just before you flew out the open bedroom window, and I texted the picture to my mother. Below it I wrote: *What kind of bird is this? Tell me. Tell me.* Mom texted back quick: *Phoenix. Definitely. Those are rare.* And I jumped out the window as the room became flames.

Opposite Day

Singing lullabies to restless kittens.
Mowing lawns with solar-powered
lawnmowers. Hang-gliding with the
homeless. It was opposite day, and I
was happy for once.

THE SON WILL BURN YOU, EVENTUALLY

They led them to an outdoor courtroom in a junkyard. The old judge sat atop a stack of crushed convertibles and glared at them. The sun glared off all the cracked and broken glass. They glared at each other, their eyes filled with both blame and love. The judge said, "How do you plead?" The man winked at the woman and she winked back, and the man said, "Our plea is to please get this over with." The woman said, "We finally agree on something." They held hands and the rude boys in the studded leather masks kicked them into the compactor. The four walls of the machine squeezed them apart, together. Elsewhere, a wild child chewed through early thoughts of reprisal and an oversized teething ring.

I Can See Paradise

Zero stars in the movie-review sky. We acted like timid actors taking acting classes on the web. You said, "I don't think it'll break." I lied, "I've seen pictures." I thought of the look on my mother's face when she found me on my knees, my body in soft spasm over the silky woman in the camping catalogue. The woman wore short shorts and a beige shirt and a red bandana. I'd leaned in and cocked my head, believing I could find more skin. The tent itself was pink and perfectly pitched. Admirable. I'd torn the page in shame and then rushed from my home, never to return. I wanted tonight to be different, though. I wanted to come and stay, to rush into your pink seams and build a home using all of our strong hands for all time always. But first: this darkness and this slippery sheepskin with only the fire in your eyes to guide me.

There Was Even a Pony

You turned on the faucet, and the water looked grainy and out of focus. We argued when I told you I needed to meet a man at the Marriott for drinks. "Just business. No funny stuff," I said. You were worried about my blackouts. I was worried, too. If only I'd known the tumor in my brain was malignant. If only I'd remembered to say, "I really like you," one last time. Outside, the world was thick with a fog that took me in like a birthday party, all cheers and backslaps and frosting stabbed with fear.

Sans Sensei

He'd constructed a sensory deprivation tank out of old washing machine parts and a children's pool. He didn't have anyone to monitor it, so he walked to the corner store and asked a group of teens who among them wanted to make some money. One raised an eyebrow, but the rest raised a hand. "Whoever guesses what I'm thinking right now gets it." He pointed to the closest teen. "Go." "A bear." "No. Next." "A bear on a roller coaster." "No. Next. And it has nothing to do with a bear." The teen who'd raised an eyebrow stepped forward, took the longest pull on the shortest cigarette, exhaled, coughed, coughed some more, then stared dead into the man's face. "It has everything to do with a bear." There was a long silence, and then the man pressed a twenty into every open palm to make this silence even longer. The way he saw it, over the long term, his senses would be deprived one way or another: with or without witnesses. The way he saw it, he didn't want to see it. He closed his eyes and pictured his sensei picturing him. He knew that it wouldn't be long now.

Somewhere in the Starburst

We began hearing rumors of Bald Casanova just after my daughter disappeared on a failed field-hockey expedition in the sequel to South Dakota. This Bald Casanova was said to be the man from the Mr. Clean bottle incarnate, except ten years younger and better dressed. Other theories held that he was the ghost of Yul Brynner returned to seduce our women into a Siamese afterlife with the promise of a smokeless ashtray and a co-starring role on the Hollywood Walk of Fame. Still, I had to consider logistics. I had to separate myself from my study of quantum chromodynamics, even though it was my job. But just the thought of catching the smarmy outline of Bald Casanova, black and backlit against a supernova, well, it made me want to fight that light as hard as I could. Maybe I'd spot my daughter somewhere in the starburst. Maybe I'd burst onto the scene with guns blazing. Maybe, with my chin tucked into my chest and my baby tucked under my arm, I'd finally get the call that it's okay to come home.

Our Own Little Private Party

The tickets were out of our price range.
You said, "Who needs to go to an End
of the World party anyway?"

Our Finest Crime

Moonlight ricocheted off the lake. We heard dogs in the distance. You smiled at me. The man in our hands went limp. We held him under a little longer to make sure, then we stripped him of his clothes and shoved him into my old tracksuit. Robbing the high rollers in the backroom of the Bikini Lounge was my idea. Kidnapping and killing my doppelgänger was yours. We swam to the other side of the lake, then drip-dried beneath a pine bough. Across the water, the dogs barked and splashed and the men splashed and hollered. They'd tear up the corpse with buckshot for sure. They'd search for days for the loot for forever. They'd lament it all in lawn chairs, drink themselves crooked. Now the blue moon lit our skin like butane. You stood looking at me, naked, and I stood looking at you, perfect.

Beginner's Luck

We married beneath a waterfall, honey-
mooned at the end of a rainbow. We
spent the trip searching for a pot of gold,
but in the end we settled into each other.
We were beginners. This was our fate.
And on the airport shuttle, you took my
hand and explained the wisdom of time-
shares.

Return Flight

With new wedding rings on our fingers, we boarded the plane in Reno. You fought me for the aisle seat but lost. "Six hours," I said, and you said, "This Xanax will make it more like sixteen seconds." We were seated in an exit row, and the flight attendant asked if we were capable of assisting in the slim chance of an emergency. I said, "When push comes to shove, I can push and shove with the best of them." You said, "Touché," and promptly passed out. The in-flight movie was the one about the orphaned cop who's also a serial killer who gets killed by his long-lost father, but in the end it turns out that the cop and his father are actually the same person. With bourbon on my breath, drugs in my blood, and your slight nose snoring on my shoulder, I felt good. I closed my eyes and thought about how everything that was ever good was always and always was good, but then the captain interrupted that goodness when he said: "We need to perform some routine maintenance, and we're being rerouted back to our departure point. We do apologize for the inconvenience. Should have you on the ground shortly." You woke up just as the same movie started up again, and I said, "Don't bother, I already know how this one ends."

VI.

The man wants to fall in love
a million different ways.

He wants his favorite way
to be from the top of the couch onto

the couch.

THE PRETENDER

I poured a beer and listened to the woman upstairs walk around in heels. Outside, the clouds were pink with sunset. It was a damn strange skyline from my first-floor vista and even stranger still was my life living in the one-bedroom below my ex-wife. I poured another beer and pretended it'd be the last of the night. I pretended my second ex-wife was beneath me in every way. Then I pretended I wasn't a sellout like the rest. I poured another beer, blasted some Pretenders, and pretended I was the last of the independents.

The Gospel of Puke

He was the man with two-and-a-half faces. Phoenix, Arizona's Favorite Son. A true box-office chameleon. Once, in an avant-garde religious picture, he played both Jesus and Mary and even had a cameo as Pontius Pilate. It was all very stylish, though most audience members would miss the best part of the show. With the exception of stating that there was no digital Satan, the producers were super tight-lipped about how the Virgin birth scene was accomplished. Audience members with an aversion to blood were wont to faint or vomit. I wanted more popcorn.

THE LOLLIPOP GUILD BREAKS BAD

The cops were coming. Again. And so again we hid—all twenty of us—inside the kitchen cabinets. We heard the cops knock on the front door. Then we heard them smash through it. Then we heard them inside the apartment. They scuffed and laughed, occasionally falling silent to admire the finer points of our meth operation maybe, perhaps our miniature beakers or pint-sized hotplates. There was much to admire, and this police interference was nothing new. So we waited. We all waited—the cops waited, too. This time something was different, though. We waited for days, then weeks. Some of us died waiting. I couldn't help but wonder what the LPAA (Little People Association of America) would have to say about this, how the papers would report it, what kinds of punishment, if any, would be handed down. But I, too, was committed to dying in hiding like my comrades. I was well aware of what happened to little guys like me in the big house.

A Percentage of Those Who Wander Are Lost

You said time is money. I said if that were true, we'd all die bankrupt. You slapped me with a rainbow trout, then kissed me so hard my lower lip split. Later, while smoking smokeless cigarettes on the pier, we watched the horizon swallow oil tankers. "We made it," you said wistfully and I nodded, though I never really knew where I was and it was your game never to tell me.

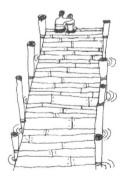

Encore

He got a nice new haircut. His laryngitis was gone. His heart hurt less and the same with his head. His surgical scars had healed. He felt like food again. Strangely, the older and deader Dad got, the more vigorous he acted. "Age is just an excuse," he said to me one night in his hospital room. "And even the high numbers are prime numbers." The next week he ran off with my wife. It was the old man's goddamn encore, but I wasn't clapping.

Last Decade

The year the world split open and bared its teeth. The year sharks grew wings and erupted from saltwater. The year the Taffy Strangler hanged himself forever to avoid trial. The year the skydivers landed on the moon on television. The year you could recognize the astronauts by their epitaphs. The year wild horsemeat was all the rage. The year the dog walkers walked themselves, and house cats hacked the Internet with their minds. The year the pursuit of happiness led to indefinite detainment. The year the humanities became the roboties. The year the nines rolled over and the clocks stopped at midnight.

The Fattest Man in the Smallest Seat

I laughed and told him I thought it might be a world record. He said, "What might be a world record, you poor fool?" I said, "Until just now, when I stumbled upon you here in that chair, I hadn't laughed in ten years." He said, "Great, get the Guinness folks on the horn and dial up a goddamn ambulance while you're at it. I can't move. Can't you see I'm stuck?" I said, "Isn't everybody?" He said, "Come here, son. Sit down. Sit on my kneecap and tell me all about it." And so I did. I sat there listing failure after failure and he sat and listened like a pro. Then, after I'd finished, he said, "Wow, that was uplifting stuff, and here I thought I had it bad. Now get the hell out of here before your dumb luck rubs off on me. Go. Now. Leave." And so I did. I was gone. But I went nowhere fast.

Hot Date with History

I dozed on the leathery backseat of Dad's Chrysler New Yorker, my face tight with whiskey. My father would be back any minute, or so he said. He needed to see a man about the future. I watched the sunset melt behind a candle factory. The moon rose and fell and dropped into the trees. I passed the time with some pills until I passed out. Dad returned at dawn, holding a box of condoms and a TV antenna. I said, "Jesus. You took forever. What's all that about?" He held up the antenna. "Son, this is the final piece of the time machine." He shook the condoms. "And these little guys will fix it to where you and your sister never happened." He tossed me the keys. "Come up here and drive," he said. "I've got a hot date with history, my boy. I need to rest. I need to sleep."

ANOTHER US

Dad said, "Son, I've got some real strange news." He said, "I've built a spaceship. Your mother and sister are gone already. We're leaving this afternoon. Can I make you a sandwich?" I said, "I'd rather have soup." Dad said, "Soup it is." Inside the spaceship, Dad worked the gears and sang 'Sweet Caroline.' Then we hit warp speed. My eyes felt like ribbons fluttering goodbye to the pinhole life in our fiery wake. We scorched gobs of dark matter. We punched through the guts of wormholes. Dad hoped he could successfully reunite us with Mom and sis. I hoped we didn't crash into ourselves coming the other way.

I Touch Yourself

The man was an enigma. He was made of puzzle pieces. No one, not even his wife, could figure him out, and one day she tired of trying and so she picked up the pieces and dumped them in the trash. The next day she felt like something was missing. A hole in her center. When she stood in front of the mirror with her shirt pulled open, she could see a whiteness, and the whiteness spoke to her. It said: "The secret to life is questioning." She said: "Did I ever love my husband?" It said: "I am your husband." She said: "That's it then." She reached into the whiteness, determined to startle its heart.

ISTANBUL

There we were, you and I and the girl, on
the balcony of our Coral Gables condo,
watching the winged sharks all swooping
and swarming and storming the beach.
You muttered something in a dead
language, so I turned away from you and
to the little blond vixen I'd been finger-
banging on the side, when she said,
"Professor, I have something to tell you."
I said, "Yes, dear. Please tell me." So she
told me, "For as long as I can remember,
I've thought science was the ultimate
arbiter of reality and that we lived but
once and died but once, and that was all,
and that was it, but now, as my time
draws near, I'm distinctly remembering
another time. It must've been Istanbul in
the rain on the pier around the time of
the invasion. I remember the soldiers
lined us up like chalk outlines minus the
chalk as they shot us, but before that, you
held me to your chest, and I distinctly
recall lipping your nipple like a cigarette.
You were my mother. I was your son. I
was two years old. I had a small erection.
We were about to die. It was all so
Freudian and fucked. It was Istanbul in
the rain on the pier in a previous life."

LET'S MAKE A DEAL (FAMILY EDITION)

Dad made me a deal: He'd give me the Firebird, but only if I promised to wreck it. He tossed me the keys. Mom made me a deal, too: She'd give me an allotment of her painkillers each week if I promised to quit stealing them. She issued me six. I took two and went for a little joyride. It was a quick trip. I crashed into an undercover cop. The Firebird became flames. And for once in my life, I made my old man proud.

VII.

The ghost of Shelby Foote wanders
into a haunted fraternity house in New Orleans.

Only to be devastated by the genuine lack of joy
to be found anywhere in the French Quarter anymore.

In life, he was haunted by the past.
In death, he's bored by the present.

No Retreat

In a coconut-themed conference room at the corporate cabana, you brought the pizza. I brought the dart gun. We were ready for the team-building exercises and the brainstorming sessions. My first idea was the best idea. I popped our supervisor, Walter, with a tranquilizer dart and said, "Okay, folks. You know the drill. What comes before Part B? Part A! That's right, it's party time." You distributed the pepperoni and magic mushroom slices and said, "Get 'em until you're gone!" Ambrose from Accounts ripped open his Hawaiian shirt and said, "It's on like Genghis Khan's mom slobbering on John Holmes' dong!" Jeanie, the office intern, produced a rum flask and passed it like a boss. Walter came-to as soon as the 'shrooms boomed. He sat up and said, "All right, I sure feel rested. I feel good. Calm. Focused. Now everyone grab a different color Sharpie and let's see if we can't get a good master list going." I said, "I'm on it." Then I tranqued him again. Everyone cheered. There was no stopping our time to shine. There was no retreating from this retreat. We were taking our talents to the streets. We'd save the company, one way or another. We were, after all, professionals.

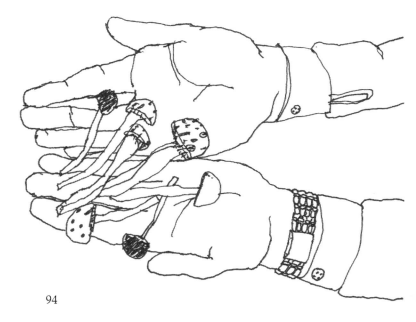

WHAT HAPPENED YESTERDAY

We flew 3,000 miles to see your mother in the ICU. It was the day after Easter. She was in a coma. Sunlight stumbled blindly through the hospital blinds and slipped on your mother's morphine drip. It stood and said: "Look at this: I packed light. Light all around. Everywhere!" You sat dazed in the chair beside the bed. The room went dark. In the corner, I watched a broken television do nothing. It was mounted to the wall like the head of a dead robot. Below the TV, a ceramic Christ hung on a little cross. It took me forever to drink a cup of instant coffee. Later, the doctor came in and discussed tomorrow.

Human Resources

It was garbage day, and we were trashed at home.

The Day Frisco Went Dark

They were debating the shock value of the electric chair they'd purchased on eBay. He was the Frank Sinatra of accordion music. She had a large inheritance and a tiny Roe v. Wade tattoo next to her naval. They had the world by the tits because the world had no balls. Hadn't had balls for a long time now. He plopped down onto the electric chair and said, "Mind if I go first? I need to get my buzz on!" A thrill-seeker to the core, she stepped barefoot and bare-legged into a pail of water and offered her hand. "How about we go together?" With a broom she swatted the breaker on the wall and immediately realized that neither of them had bothered to lower the voltage.

Inquire Within

The cat had a sixteen-dollar-a-day seafood habit. I worried about money, but I worried more about the lack of it. I talked to the cat like a confidant and friend. I said: "I feel like I have two birds fighting in my heart. One bird is an eagle. The other is a dove. Our future depends on which one wins." The cat sat in the kitchen window in the sun. It yawned and said nothing. I sat there at the empty table, listening to the screen door bang itself in the breeze. I thought I might go down to the sperm bank and apply for the security-guard gig. Earlier, I'd seen a sign in their window and now I took it as one.

CRAPS

Your eyes rolled like dice. I was feeling lucky. I was thinking sex swing. You were thinking airport. And Costa Rica. I didn't know this until Vegas. You'd known since Reginald. His fat legs straddled my neck. He sucked his pacifier. My pacifier was lost to the sky. From the ground we watched your flight fight the sunset until the sunset saw black.

What Goes Around

I'd been working the graveyard shift at the town graveyard for six weeks when bones began to sprout like flowers around the headstones. The bones grew into new people, people who didn't know the people they once were. With their new fingers, they traced their old names. I brought them blankets. I fed them soup and gave them Gatorade. I taught them math and science and literature, what little I knew. I told them I loved them, and I meant it.

Birds of Paradise

We gave each other hand jobs then went for coffee. Outside, I couldn't stop squinting. You suggested it was because my political future was bright. I thought it might have had something to do with yesterday's initiation ritual with the bird costumes and the blood-drinking contest.

Missing Person

We played candlelight charades in the coroner's living room. In the shadows I obsessed over the open-endedness of today's horoscope: Something will happen. After everyone had ten more drinks, something did happen. From the basement you brought up a redheaded Jane Doe. She filled your arms, shiny and stiff like a waxy mannequin. We all turned to the coroner who shrugged and said, "I can't help it. Sometimes I take my work home."

Size Matters

We watched the sunset from the parking lot of our sex therapist's office. You removed a golden pocket watch from your purse and attempted to hypnotize me. It didn't work, but I pretended it did. I clucked like a chicken. I barked like a dog. I banged my head against the passenger window. I banged my head against the windshield. I banged my head against the passenger window. The sun was long gone by the time I tried to fuck myself. It was great to finally hear you laugh. I was thankful for the darkness. I was more thankful for my very average-sized penis.

Bad Gift for an Insomniac

The kids didn't have much of a head start, but we were too damn drunk. You tweaked the throttle with a tiny flathead screwdriver, said, "You watching?" I said, "No, sorry." I was in my head. I was thinking about that bullshit dreamcatcher you bought me for my birthday. That's a bad gift for an insomniac. I was also thinking about the kids. We'll never catch up to them no matter how hard we try. They drive dangerously, like their entire lives are ahead of them (and they are) and they live like death isn't an option for anyone other than us, while listening to songs sung by breast implants and reading books with titles like *I Feel Like You Feel Like I Might Feel Like You Might Feel, Too*, but I don't feel anything like that anymore. I feel like the drugs I'm taking aren't working. I feel old and tired and bored. You tweaked the throttle again, and we listened to the engine die for good. You said, "Well, that's that." But it wasn't that. It was something else. It was something we could never catch.

HOMESCHOOL

Dad dropped me at the door and said he'd be back in a half-hour. I didn't see him again for fourteen years. It was graduation day.

Like library conversations canceled
by airplane thunder.

Beyond fucked and understanding.

In line at a drive-thru pharmacy.

24 / 365 / World

Baffled by our hometown's cryptic motto:

Colder Than Russian Novels

Like what the birthplace of John Randolph of Roanoke became.

24 / 365 / World

A Different House

I cut off my ponytail and put it into the box. You cut off your ponytail and put it next to mine. I put the finishing touches on the ransom note and put it in the box. If your father paid, we'd save the house. If he didn't, or if we got caught, we'd be living in a different house.

BLUE CHRISTMAS

I reached for a cigarette. You were having a seizure, but I didn't know it yet. It was Christmas Eve, and everything was quiet for once at the halfway house. The others were out caroling, and although my emphysema prohibited me from singing, it didn't stop me from smoking. I stepped onto the porch, torched a menthol, and found you seizing in the snow. Afterward, out of breath, I helped you to your feet and said, "Your seizure almost gave me a heart attack." You lied and said it wasn't a seizure. You said you were making an angel in the snow. I scrutinized the wild pattern and said, "That looks more like a snow demon." "Yes, sir," you said. "That there is the one and only Snow Angel of Death, and it's coming for us all someday, but this is my time now and I'll have to go it alone." In the distance, I could hear the men singing 'White Christmas' and I noticed you were turning blue.

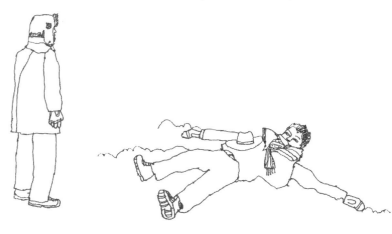

E = N∪DE∞

I'm nude because I'm not wearing any clothes. They were stripped off me, after work, by a marauding pack of strippers. Now I'm free, though not because I'm not wearing any clothes, but because I've figured out the formula, and somewhere in that damn laboratory, or perhaps it was some time—some swirling, quantum toilet—something dawned, a morning, or a morning on a night, a night filled with full moons and laughter and convertibles, a tripped-out black-light erasure on a basement wall, something by Bill Blake maybe, all the kids sitting cross-legged on the indoor/outdoor carpet, arms locked, fingers interlocked, heads knocked back, and all of them all-knowing, and nude, like me, because yes, they were, for certain, not wearing any clothes at all. Such was my beginning, long before my funding for Antarctica, long before those strippers grazed my sagging skin with their chests, breasts, and hearts. I told them, "This is happening now," and since their painted lips were splashed between worlds they could not think to otherwise mutter, or spark.

109

Vacation from Vacation

We missed our freeway exit and ended up
at a defunct hospital. From the backseat
came a cluster of cocksuckers and mother-
fuckers. Then we missed the on-ramp and
had to turn around at an abandoned airport. In the rearview I glared at the twins
glaring at me and mouthed 'Bring it,
boys!' You searched your purse for breath
mints but returned with sleeping pills.
"Cheers," you said. "Wake me up in
Arizona." The twins said, "I want one! I
want one!" And you gave them two each.
Soon enough the backseat was snoring. I
cracked the window and lit a joint. I
thought about driving straight through to
the Grand Canyon. Then I thought about
driving straight into the Grand Canyon.
Then I rolled up the window and thought
better of it. It was too dark outside to
think dark thoughts. When we crossed the
state line I whispered, "Arizona." Then
your head was in my lap, and my lap was
in your mouth. My hands relaxed on the
wheel, and my eyes relaxed on the road,
the road. The road kept coming.

LITTLEST BIG MAN

He'd never tried to swim. Until now.
The ocean visibly cringed at the sight
of his airborne cannonball. He was
borne through generations of whiskey
and elongated bone. He was borne
through miles of kite-running and
speed-walking and jobs-stopping. He
squeezed his knees to his small chest.
There was an impact. As the water
wall rose, the world tucked and turned,
one eye open, hidden grin.

THE NEXT ROOM

My mother was in the next room. I'd
had a wild dream about God I meant to
write down. I'd just woken up. It'd
already been a long day. My mother was
on her deathbed. It was a futon. She was
in the next room. I'd found God in a
dream. My mother thought everyone
she met was a saint. She saw their potential. I'd just woken up. It'd already been
a long day. I was waiting for something
to happen. I wrote down my dream. I'd
just woken up. I was waiting for something to happen. My mother was on her
deathbed. It was a futon. She was in the
next room. Everyone she met was a
saint. She saw their potential. I'd just
woken up. It'd already been a long day.
I was waiting for something to happen.
It did.

GROUP THERAPY

He fought depression. He beat his wife's boyfriend.

Ground Rules

On Monday the cat pissed in the plant. I put the plant outside. On Tuesday the cat pissed on the bathmat. I put the bathmat in the trash. On Wednesday the cat pissed in its litter box, and things went according to plan. On Thursday the cat pissed in the house. I put the cat outside. Friday I couldn't find the cat. Saturday I still couldn't find the cat. This lasted for many months. Then one night I got real drunk and stayed that way for weeks. I felt so bad about the cat. When I sobered up, I managed to lock myself out. I put my foot through some glass and broke in. There was the cat asleep on the bed. I woke him up and said: "Fancy seeing you here. I've been looking for you everywhere, and here you are. Now let's get something straight. We're going to need to set some ground rules. I'm going to show you something important. I'm going to show you how it's done." Then I went over to his litter box and pissed in it and wept.

Songs for a Better Life

We took a wrong turn and ended up hooked on heroin. Then we took another wrong turn and ended up on the freeway. It turned into a dried-up river-bed that was longer than a holiday weekend. The conversation we had was so far beneath us. We were high as balsa-wood flyers. You searched the stations for a better song. I searched the riverbed for answers. Nothing. We were going somewhere once. Children. A mortgage. Tuscaloosa. It seemed that now we were just waiting for the dam to crack in the rearview and for the river-bed to fill. The icy surge would surely overtake us and the mangy H we rode in on.

APParition

She sat on the porch and introduced herself as Marcy. I said, "Marcy?" She said, "No, Mercy." I said, "Mercy?" She said, "No, Merci. M, E, R, C, I." Even with her sitting down, you could tell she was tall. She wore an old bathrobe over a sequined dress. I took a drag from my cigarette and said, "That's an interesting name. Is it French?" She said, "Silence. I'm here to help you help yourself, you fool." Then a rainbow beam blasted from her forehead and turned my cigarette into a bird. The bird shat on my shirt and flew off into the night. I was scared. She stood and said, "Fear is the opposite of truth. Be honest." She was tall, taller than a small forward. She opened her robe and revealed four caped dwarves praying on their knees. She said, "Never mind them. Look at me. Eyes up here. Listen: You will stop gambling on horseracing and high school basketball games. You will start saving. You will stop smoking. You will start jogging. You will stop drinking. You will start juicing. You will quit your day job. You will teach yourself to code. You will invent an app that projects a hologram of me and gives advice. You will call it APParition. You will make millions. You will donate half to charities of your choice. After a gala event, you will impregnate an equine veterinarian. You will move to Tucson, and together you will raise a child prodigy and care for hundreds of horses." I said, "But I hate horses." She said, "You will learn to love them, and they will bring you unbridled joy." I said okay, and suddenly I felt okay. She said, "Yes, from now on you will never feel the same about your feelings again." And then I didn't, but then I did.

Pickup Artists

By midday our tiny home had filled with tradesmen. I jockeyed for room to make us peanut butter sandwiches. It wasn't easy. Still, we tried to take it easy, knowing that nothing worth doing was ever stress-free. All afternoon we sat there freeing our stresses as best we could, chasing pretzels with Schlitz as the walls tumbled around us. After sunset, when the men finally knocked off for the day, they'd already knocked down the partitions and installed two pine lanes and a ball return. And before the foreman left, he said, "We'll be back to mount the pinsetter machine in the morning. After that: the projectors. You'll be in business by the end of the week." I said, "Good, because the wife and I can't wait to start working from home."

It's Not Easy Being Green Cheese

I'd been measuring the months in unpaid bills and prepaid calling cards (although no one answered the phone anymore when I called), existing in an endless interval between upstart shutdowns and Powerball winners. This morning I skipped the mirror and went out into the world. The world had decided to skip me, I realized, when my foot fell into a puddle of dark matter and kept on falling. I ended up eating lunch on the dark side of the moon, mooning nosy satellites and tossing bread crusts to less finicky and more likeable cosmic cowgirls. I longed for longer relationships, a sense of balance, the perfect cup of coffee. What I got instead was a spectacular view of galaxies slow-motion salsa dancing, and I guess I can think of worse ways to spend a few lifetimes.

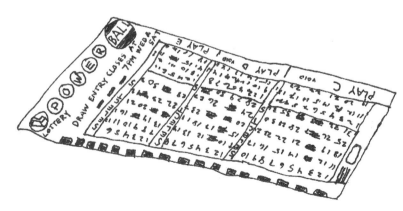

IX.

After the game, we tarnished ourselves
with Maker's Mark & ginger ale.

Then we lit out for the suburbs.

Passing Mild West Mortgages and E-Z Street Loans.

Marooned at Pedestrian X-Way.

We put our faith in Henry Ford and look what it's done.

Jaywalking is damn near impossible.

Just ask the North American deer.

Magic Hour

Our outdoor training session was interrupted by a pride parade. The old man flinched. "Hold fire," he said, and by fire he meant steel. It was Knife Night at the gun club, and we were rationing our ammo and practicing our pitching. I'd brought along six switchblades and a big bag of steak knives. The old man was working with a set of samurai swords: stabbing and slicing the cardboard silhouettes to shit. Me? I'd been lucky enough to introduce several movie-star posters to a few Chinese stars. And then along came the Dykes on Bikes and the double-decker rainbow buses and the S&M floats and balloons and bears and a pink submarine and briefs, thousands of men in briefs. The old man put down his swords and pulled down his pants. He said, "There are two kinds of people in this world: those who watch the parade and those who join." He ripped off his shirt and hopped on the back of a party bus. He waved as he receded into the distance. The sky seemed strange. It was the hour they called magic hour.

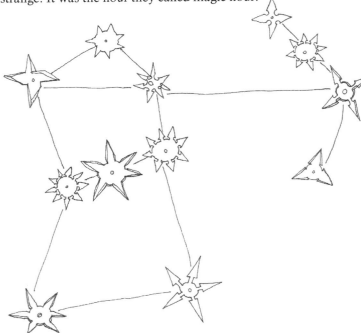

Everything That Was Ever Wrong

I filled up the flask and hightailed it down to the beach at high tide and shouted, "Come on!" Then I drained the flask and waited. Then I drained my bladder and waited. A seagull. A seagull. An old man with a metal detector, sweeping over the sand with the metal detector, never touching the sand with his metal detector. A seashell. I picked up the seashell and put it to my ear. I needed to make a call. I hoped you'd answer, but all I got was the pounding sound of everything that was ever wrong.

Keys

You said: "I can't do it anymore." I said: "Don't." And then we didn't and then we didn't and then we did. After we did, you said: "Keys." I tossed them to you, dressed, and left. Outside, I fired up the old riding mower and headed toward beer or liquor, whichever came first.

SANCTUARY

People ask about the birds, and it's my job to tell them. I'm not only a tour guide at the state bird sanctuary; I'm also a published poet and there's nothing more poetic than a bird flying by and making you feel stupid. There's a nice dramatic irony there, too, when a bird flies by and makes you feel stupid because birds are the stupid ones. No, it's true. They're not smart at all. They have brains the size of peanuts. Yes, some days I stand around feeding those stupid bastards peanuts and thinking about how poetic and strange it is to be feeding these peanut-brains peanuts, and then the birds fly off and I feel stupid again. But I'm not stupid. I've read *Ulysses* by Joyce Carol Oates, and I can recite from memory *The Red Wheelbarrow* by Old Carlos Santana. I'm not stupid at all, you stupid fucking birds! That's right. You better fly away. Fly away because you're free. I like to go to rock concerts and drink too much and call out "Freebird!" between songs because it's a free country and I can say what I want when I drink too much at a rock concert, so I say "Freebird!" between songs and then I feel as free as a bird. I feel like I could fly away from it all, and then the next day I'm back here at the bird sanctuary, hung over. People asking me about these goddamn birds. I usually just make stuff up: Catbird, Dogbird, Philadelphia Eagle. The truth is I don't know anything about birds. Now if you ask me about flowers, I can tell you a fuck-ton about flowers. All my poems are about flowers. Why flowers? Because all the real poets are pushing daisies these days and I take sanctuary in that.

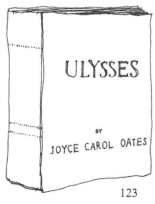

A New Kind of Hump Day

I caught the new guy breakdancing in the break room. I needed to add some coffee to my Kahlúa. He noticed me standing in the doorway. He was in the middle of a backspin. I nodded, and he spun to a stop with his knees to his shoulders and his mouth just inches from his crotch. I said: "Hey." And he said: "Hey." And I said: "Hey, that was pretty good. I need to get my day started." I raised my mug. He raised his eyebrows and lowered his crotch to his mouth. He mumbled: "Me, too." And I said: "Oh." We both looked the other way, but all the Kahlúa in the world can't help me unsee what I saw. For years now I've been trying to reenact that beautiful image, but I just don't have the tools. My breakdancing days were over before they started. I've always been more of a polka person.

Immortality Sucks

Outside the new antique store, we were getting multi-generational with our momma jokes, offering great-grandmother slurs to nervous passers-by while eying great-grandfather clocks through bulletproof glass and lapping up vanilla ice cream cones. We felt like we could go on forever. Sadly, we did.

My Head My Voice
My Shoes My Toes

We took the kids to the Counterfeit
Museum. They had a replica of the first
copy machine, but it didn't replicate. They
had bowls of plastic fruit, and the fruit
was dimpled with teeth marks. They had
currency from "all over the world," but it
all looked like Monopoly money. The
money got me thinking about how we met
over that game of strip Monopoly and
how, after I took all but your panties and
you took my everything, we scrambled to
the rooftop and swallowed MDMA pills
and then a bottle of whiskey and then
each other and then the night. With our
new wings, we pounded around satellites
and stars and planets. It was after school
and before jobs and marriage and kids. It
was the last time in my life I wasn't
stretched thin. I was compact but weight-
less. I was alive and filled with my own
blood. I was a diamond, a real one. Then
the boy with your soft blue eyes and my
floppy ears tugged my hand to go to the
next display, something with the movie
Blade Runner running on a loop. I said,
"Wait, I'm not finished here yet." And in
my head my voice sounded far away, but
in my shoes, my toes were already feeling
for solid ground.

Fair's Fair

Some fuck started a fire on our street.
We passed out with Midnight Oil on
the turntable. If the question is *How can
we sleep when our beds are burning?* then
the answer is: fair enough.

Cowboy Candy

I punched the jukebox, literally. I couldn't stand country music on principle. Then I couldn't stand up. All around me, rednecks got down to Garth Brooks. Then some redneck went down on me to Kacey Musgraves. I swear I felt God, and God's tongue was rough like sandpaper. Rough like Daddy's stubble. Rough like you used to be back when you gave a shit. Back when I wasn't splayed out like some kind of cowboy candy. Back when I was an upstanding man who could still stand up.

Fireworks

After the fireworks we danced in the living room. The neighbors called the cops. I called the cops, too. I called them a couple of fascist bastards, and they kicked down the door. Then there were more fireworks.

Ultimate Ultimatum

I hid in the bathroom and read the backs of shampoo bottles until lunchtime. I had guns stashed all over the house. Cops outside. Crops inside. My manifesto was getting lots of likes on Facebook, and my Twitter followers had shot to triple digits in the few hours since I'd issued my ultimate ultimatum. I demanded things. Things like: Amnesty. Freedom to grow. Six pizzas and a six-pack. A quick lick job from that Lohan chick. A Chick-fil-A sandwich or two. A quart of rum. A quarter of a million dollars wired to an account in the Caribbean. A friend to raise hell with on weekends. My old man to burn in hell. A helicopter. A Cessna. A carpool full of single mothers. A legion of lawyers. A slimmer shadow. Ultimately though, I demanded a sustainable solution to global warming by morning. Else the hostage gets it, I said. Farewell. Goodbye. Now, you can say that a man who takes himself hostage in his own home and drops a dime to the local news channel (which actually wasn't all that interested) is a man without a plan. You could also say that a man without a plan wouldn't own so many weapons, and you wouldn't be wrong.

American Adventure

We pitched a fit. Then we pitched
our tents in the hotel lobby. The way
I saw it we were like our American
Adventure cabin coupon: innocent
until proven unredeemable, and I'd
never felt more born.

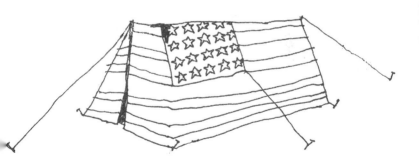

The thrift store beside the church is open.
The man needs long-sleeved shirts.

The woman needs to see whether
they have any hats she likes.

After they make guns with their hands
and pretend to shoot holes in the ground,

an old man sitting on his front porch
shows them his toothless smile.

Fresh Air

By today's standards he was a relic. For instance, he'd never once used his camera phone to take a dong-o-gram. He'd never savored a Cosmic Brownie. He'd never even learned the basics of string theory. How did the man expect to walk through walls? Was it our job to feel bad for him, or to encourage him through a few night classes? My eyes were aching from all this stress, and I couldn't see what you were doing to yourself. When I told you I wasn't interested, I meant exactly that. No amount of goodwill could've changed how I felt. My heart hurt less when there was just one window open in the house.

Recovery

After draining the toilet, I put everything in the toilet. I drank a bottle of cough syrup and went outside. The cat spoke to birds. The birds spoke to bees. The bees spoke to me. They swarmed in proximity to my head and said, "A culture of rampant sexual repression and misogyny promotes chaos and leads to collective violence and insanity. The veil will soon be lifted. The fourth dimension is upon us, a realm of pure consciousness constituted by a democratic and communal mind. See you there. Don't be late." The bees dropped to the ground and died, and then came one of those epiphanic moments where everything was clear and the trajectory of my future crystallized in a single thought: store. I went to the store and picked up a forty of Olde English, a box of menthols, and a Shake Weight. "Health kick?" the clerk asked. I nodded and left without paying. Yes, I had all the instruments now for an absolute recovery.

The Rare Undetectable Humantopus

They took me to the radar room. I saw everything except myself. It was a huge relief. They
said, "It's true. You *are* one of them." I said,
"No shit. And in a minute y'all will be one of
us, too." They gasped when I slipped out of
my restraints. They moaned when I slipped
out of myself and into their soft parts. My
tentacles were many. My suction was undeni-
able.

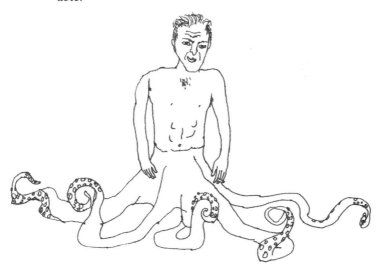

Afterlife Insurance

It was raining animals, and we sweated nude in the glass-walled parlor of my attorney's home in the hills. We counted and recounted my newly acquired old money into thick stacks in the corner. I'd hit big on a superfecta, and then I'd hit on a small cocktail waitress and now we were celebrating with absinthe and LSD at my lawyer's house on the best side of midnight. He was out of the country. I was out of my mind. We finished the bottle then finished counting the money. Half was in the fireplace. "Why are we burning this?" she said. "Seems like a waste." "Nonsense," I said. "This is the best money you'll never spend. Not only are we repaying the debts of our ancestors, but we're also taking out a little afterlife insurance. This money will wait for us in the next world." "In that case," she said, "we'd better burn it all, including our credit cards."

Temp-to-Fire Agency

I was working as a personal assistant's personal assistant. My job was to catch everything that fell through the cracks. I was commended after Chester Goldbaum's tear-stained men's room Devil confession. I quit after Susan Ortega's baby chewed its way out of Susan Ortega and into my backpack. For fifteen bucks an hour, there's a finite number of super-natural cataclysms a mind can process, and mine stopped at Antichrist.

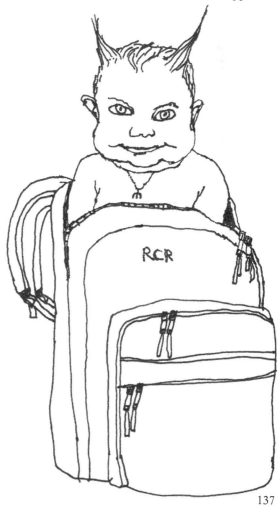

Can't Catch Karma

I studied the labels of beer cans and stared through the open kitchen window. So much cattle in this bullshit world. It was seven a.m. It was time to go to work. On the road I asked the Lord for a sign. I said: "Something, anything, old man. Come on." A mile or so later, I saw an Amber Alert and thought: This is my time to shine. I'll castrate that freak on the side of the road. I'll be a hero. I always wanted to be one. Then it dawned on me that I was driving the same make and model as this pervert and that the license plate matched my own. But how could this be? I'd purchased the thing fair and square on Craigslist a few months ago. Paid cash. Plus, I was alone in this world, and my children were grown. Hadn't had a conversation with anyone other than God in a week. I reached into the passenger seat and cracked another cold one. I saw the red flashing lights in the rearview and decided not to pull over. Those state boys would have to catch me. And you can't catch karma. It catches you.

Beat Too Long

The cult leader leaned into the microphone and said: "Welcome home, newbs! Some ground rules: (1) Everybody have fun tonight. (2) Everybody Wang Chung tonight." You said: "I think we're going to like it here!" I said: "Is that a pig-man?" You said: "Yeah!" I said: "Let's fuck it!" You said: "What?" I said: "Yeah! Let's fuck it!" You said: "Oh! That's what I thought you said! I'm tired of porking!" I said: "Oh! Me, too!" It took me an extra beat to say anything, though, which, as it turned out, was a beat too long. Now you were seated at the right hand of the leader, licking his toes, ankles, knees, thighs, and then his—and I knew right then that I needed to revise my idea of fun.

Johnny Depp Prepares for His Role as Raoul Duke

By the end of the first day, I had the accent down cold. By the end of the second day, I could mimic your movements. By the end of the week, I'd cleaned your garage and polished your guns. By the end of the next, I was wearing your clothes and smoking your drugs. By the end of the month, it felt like a year. By the end of the year, it felt like 1971. We were heading toward Vegas, stoned. On our way to find the American Dream in action. On our way to the Criterion Collection.

Proof through the Night

After the game there was another game. After that, the remaining members of Three Dog Night took the field with hula hoops and harmonicas. The crowd groaned, booed. Beneath the bleachers we saw the team manager's youngest, a pale-faced boy named Crick. He was wearing a three-piece suit and slicking his hair back with pine-needle pomade. He smiled at us and gathered himself into a tight formation. He snapped off a short series of salutes, and then he showed us a briefcase full of uranium. You said, "That kid's going places." I pushed out my bottom lip and nodded. I turned my attention back to the darkening field, to the uninspired music, and to whatever patriotic dishonesty came next.

THE POWER OF PIE COMPELS YOU

When it was over, you appeared on the porch. You appeared relieved. I said, "I won't ask." You said, "Dad wants pizza, and he wants you to get it." You turned back toward the cabin but stopped and said, "Buy a shovel and five gallons of gas. Things didn't go well for the exorcist." Then you sighed and your demeanor shifted to make me feel nervous. In a voice I mostly recognized you said, "Focus on the pizza first. Dad, he really wants some goddamn pizza."

College Algebra

You took down the big one while I watched. We both took down the small ones at the same time. Then the waitress brought out two more big ones and we both took down the big ones and ordered two more small ones, and when she brought the small ones, we took them down. We paid, stood up, and you fell down. I helped you up, but you couldn't get up, so I sat back down and ordered another round. The waitress brought out two more big ones and we took them down and ordered two more small ones, and when she brought the small ones, we took them down. We paid, stood up, and you fell down. I helped you up, but you couldn't get up, so I sat back down and ordered another round. Later, the night blurred into years and now the hard math is ahead. If the above is true, how many big ones and small ones did we take down?

BEER

After Breakfast

We found eagle bones stacked on the welcome mat. Shotgun fire on the answering machine. You were amazed at my landline. I was blown away by the percussion grenades that dropped on your lawn like outfield bloops. You cradled my head in your lap. My body was all over the neighborhood. You said I died with a smile on my face. I said I died knowing one last good summer.

XI.

The Ghost of Shelby Foote roams
the American landscape
until he hits the mountains
and stops at a meditation retreat in Aspen.

Only to be overcharged and underwhelmed.

The crowd is so into themselves
that they don't even notice a dead historian in their midst.

They're too busy discussing the value of silence.

The Setup

I arrived with a gym bag full of PCP. You arrived with a gym bag full of cigarette cartons. I said, "We can set up over here." You said, "The setup started years ago." You flashed a badge, and lightning came down in the form of a pistol butt and struck me between the eyes. The last thing I remember was choking to sleep on a slice of pavement pie. Years later, tethered to the cold rails with hot blood in your mouth, the last thing you remembered was how you always cheated to win because I didn't know how to lose.

BROKE AND BROKER

You broke my heart. I broke your
windows. I went broke paying to
fix your broken windows. I went
broker attempting to fix my broken
heart with anything illegal.

Vanishing Act

Your water broke backstage. Behind the curtain the crowd roared. You said we still had enough time to do the show, so we did the show. We started with the Flaming Sword Cabinet bit and transitioned into card tricks, and then I escaped from a straitjacket while you juggled kitchen knives in the corner. "And for my next trick," I said, "I will saw a woman in half, and not just any woman, a pregnant woman." You lay flat on the table. I fired up the circular saw. You screamed and screamed. This wasn't part of the act. The crowd gasped. I stopped the saw and walked around to your legs and lifted your skirt. "Oh," I said. "I see. I'm going to need a volunteer from the audience ASAP. Is there a doctor in the house? She's having a baby!" A man leaped onto the stage and told you to breathe. He said, "Just breathe." He said, "You're doing fine." He said, "It's crowning." He said, "Here it comes." He said, "Congratulations. It's a girl." The crowd went wild. I fired up the circular saw, cut the cord, and handed you the baby. The crowd went wilder. Then I fired up a cigar and disappeared. Years later, you told me it was my worst trick.

All Talk and No Follow-Through

The flight attendant told us we were now allowed to use our portable electronic devices. The man next to me pulled out a miniature time machine he didn't know how to use yet. I knew it was a miniature time machine because I'd built it two thousand years before. I also knew how this flight would end: on a damp tarmac in Texas after a lousy film starring that guy who's in everything. And I knew how this world would end: smothered by too many beginnings.

MISSING CHILDREN

You poured a shot and then poured your heart out. Outside, the rain poured and poured. I stood at the window watching the kid across the cul-de-sac shooting free throws in the rain. The rain fell sideways and the wind picked up and the kid hit six straight shots and you hit me in the arm and asked me what we should do and I said I'd have to think about it. I poured myself a shot, tossed it back, and thought about it. I didn't know much about much. The kid missed a layup. I missed Mississippi. You missed the children we'd never had.

THE FIRST SUPPER

I threw a party. You threw a punch. I caught the punch with my nose. My nose didn't want the punch, but there was nowhere else to put it. Things had been breaking down like this for some time. Everything was looking for space, but space was sick of everything. The answer was obvious, but no one would admit it: It was time to put our guns down and go home, collect our sashes from pot-bellied oaks, and press our own pot bellies into American dinner tables. We'd pull and scoot and scoot and pull until our blind fingers slipped past the flap and flicker of stiff tablecloths to find warm, familiar skin finding us underneath.

Hell's Kitchen

In the distance, the roar of motorcycles and an explosion of heavy metal. I said, "Maybe the dumbest thing you ever did was admitting to these dudes that you knocked over their bikes." You said, "It was the right thing to do. Besides, they saw me do it. You'd prefer a dead wife? Now get the dogs on the grill and the ice in the cooler. They'll be here any minute." I said, "How many more nights of this nonsense?" You said, "The deal was one meal for every bike. You know this. I don't know. Ten more times?" I said, "Goddammit." You said, "Watch it." By the time I got the grill going, the front yard looked like a used Harley dealership. Beards and bandanas all around. Leather everywhere. The neighbors locked their doors and closed their blinds. I opened the cooler and tossed a beer to God Boss, to Forrest Gimp, to Chocolate Thunder, to Boner Jammer, to Little Eddie, to Jerry the Junky, to Texas Toast, to Marvin Straight, to Dirty Dickless, to Not-So-Fast Franky, and to at least a dozen more. God Boss cracked his beer and inquired about tonight's menu, and I told him hotdogs and sauerkraut and homemade kale salad. Little Eddie took issue with the salad. I said, "Look Little Eddie, there's no bitchin' in this kitchen. Besides, you need to eat your greens. They'll make you big and strong, and if you keep eating those vegetables, they'll be calling you Big Eddie before long." Little Eddie told me to eat shit and die and then God Boss smacked him on the back of the head and the others whistled and cheered and for a moment I felt like an insider among outlaws and then you came outside.

TRUE STORY

I was walking down the street and there
was a parrot in a window and it said,
"Hello." And I said, "Hello." And it said,
"Hello." And I said, "Hello." And it said,
"Hello." And I said, "Goodbye." And it
said, "Goodbye." And it said, "Goodbye." And it said, "Goodbye."

Dust Bowling

We were fifty miles outside of nowhere when we sobered up.
You said, "Henry." And I said, "Curtis." We laughed, hung
our heads, shook hands, and agreed to try again as soon as
possible. We believed that eventually we'd sober up to be
different people. For now, though, we had just enough money
to catch the bus to the next dust-bowl town, the next dust-bowl
bowl of stew, the next dust-bowl bowling alley where, hope-
fully, we could score some jobs long enough to fuel our next
blackout bender. Yeah, it's true we didn't have much. We had
our goal and we'd always have each other, at least until one of
us bowled the perfect game that brought more beer, glory, and
blinding light than a dust-bowl life could take.

September 10, 2001

The ocean took your top. I took
your picture. That night, we took
each other's born-again virginity. It
was the end of our honeymoon.

WE TOOK OUR TIME

It was a matter of fact. Or it was a matter of factions. We couldn't quite tell. Regardless, it was time for action so we suited up in our homemade riot gear and body armor. We took to the streets, and then we took the streets. We took to the city, and then we took the city. We lopped off the heads of false prophets and slammed them onto spikes. We burned effigies of past and present leaders. We read paperbacks on the tops of skyscrapers and filled our portable electronic devices with saltwater. It was like this everywhere. At dawn we all stood shoulder to shoulder and pissed a giant circle around the world. Those who could wag their genitalia wagged their genitalia, and those who couldn't wiggled their hips. We'd done it. We'd really done it. We'd finally taken our time, which was all we ever wanted. The moon pushed beneath the horizon and rang like the close of the second round of a fight scheduled for fifteen.

LIFE AFTER COMA

Whoa, fresh-out-of-the-dryer jeans. Whoa, blueberry pancakes. Whoa, coffee brewing. Whoa, extra-spicy Bloody Mary. Whoa, mild sedative. Whoa, baseball on the radio. Whoa, football on TV. Whoa, leather couches. Whoa, bare feet on carpet. Whoa, open windows. Whoa, curtains blowing in the breeze. Whoa, this place feels like a stranger's house but more comfortable. Whoa, everything seems so electric and alive. Whoa, it's almost like the appliances are breathing. Whoa, if I think too much I get a headache and my nose bleeds. Whoa, I can't remember who I was or who I wasn't or what I did or what I didn't do. Whoa, it doesn't matter now, does it? Whoa, my lawyer says I'm set for life. Whoa, my wife says she's so happy I'm home. Whoa, my wife is smoking a cigarette. Whoa, I didn't think anyone still smoked cigarettes. Whoa, that isn't a cigarette. Whoa, can I get a hit? Whoa, I must be dreaming. Whoa, I hope I don't wake up. Whoa, whoa, whoa.

The man and the woman don't ride in hot-air balloons.
They see them when they run.

They don't see them
all the time.

Wait.
Follow my finger.

There.

LIGHT EATERS

After dinner we went for a walk. You wanted to see the lunar eclipse. I did, too, so I thought we'd get a better look. We stopped at the abandoned drive-in since it was on one of the highest hilltops. Long ago, the place had been called the Starlight Theater, but now there were letters missing and the sign said: light eater. You said that the sign was a sign that you needed to return to your wheatgrass regimen. I said that the sign was a great idea for a New Age death cult: The Light Eaters. "Imagine it," I said. "If all you ate was light, you wouldn't last long." You disagreed and pointed to the horizon. "You could make it awhile, I think, months maybe, before you'd need anything else." I traced an invisible line from your finger to the sky. The moon looked like a dark disc with light leaking from it. I felt a pain in my gut, and I was hungrier than hell.

Tomorrow, We'll Be Rested

Tonight I was drunker than drunk with all the librarians in Texas partying hard in my backyard. My wife said, "This is something special going on right here. This is tragic." She spit her beer back into her beer and said, "This is me leaving you for another woman. This is the beginning of the end, and the end of the worst sitcom in American history. This is muckraking, and you're the muck." Now the bonfire of Bibles in our yard had begun to grow and the flames threatened to singe the low-hanging stars. My wife threatened custody if I didn't scram. She told me to leave. Now. Go. I took your small hand and helped you beneath the barbed wire and into the neighboring pasture. We stood on the sleepy spines of upright cattle and tried to pluck every perfect idea from the sky. Yes, we wanted to finish what we started. We wanted to sleep in our own beds, and for once, we wanted to wake up in a world that didn't seem shot.

The Opposite of Forgettable

I met her at the Marriott bar. She said her name was Fancy, which must've been a fake, and she was the opposite of forgettable with her neck like a hotel sculpture. She said her name like she meant it. She said she sang opera for fun. She said she was an underwater fashion photographer. I ordered another rum punch and asked if she enjoyed her job. She flashed a derringer in her palm and asked if I liked parlor tricks. She bit her lip quick, and it bled into red lipstick. When I shrugged she upped the ante and asked whether I enjoyed my life. I said, "Depends." Then I said, "You're not an underwater photographer, are you?" She put her pistol back in her purse and said, "I can't even swim," which was all well and good because I could drink and swim like a fish, and considering I'd just dosed myself with Mad Hatter someone would have to navigate when we went off the deep end together.

OUR OLD SKINS

For better or worse had worsened to the point of pointlessness. Now we had to do what we had to do. We had to reach back to the beginning, pull off our costumes, and pull on our old skins. We had to rid ourselves of electronics and paint Black Friday red. We had to buy a drum of paint and a broken war drum that could only play peace. We had to position ourselves on high ground and press our feet into the mud. We had to purge ourselves of daylight. We had to bleed ourselves of fear. We had to close our eyes and sing into familiar mouths. We had to love wide open.

How We Came to Live at the Naked Buffalo Casino Ranch Resort Desert Commune despite Our Best Intentions and Because of Our Worst Impulses

It was time to go home.
We tried.

MAGGIE

My sister's girlfriend carved up the bird. It was Thanksgiving. She asked if I was a breast man or a thigh man. I thought about it and said, "Neither. I'm a vagina man." Then I went back to cleaning my guns. My Beretta was a heart man. My Mustang was a pocket man. My .44 Magnum was a woman. Margaret was her name, but I always called her Maggie.

SEARCH PARTY

The fog had grown heavier, and we only had one hour of light to cover three miles. I walked with the new guy, Jerry, the messiest orderly I'd ever seen. He had eyes like shiny new shovels, and I suspected he dug deep into the pharmacy stash when no one was looking. He was, after all, the reason we were in this mess. We staggered through rows of old redwoods and California laurels, over streams shriveled to muck. A mile or so later, we came to a clearing, smelled strong cannabis, and saw what appeared to be the missing patients, crouching in the shadow of a sequoia. They waved nonchalantly, as if it were standard procedure to meet each other here. Jerry cracked his knuckles and crossed his arms. I said, "All right, you two. Party's over. Let's go." The one who was holding the joint passed it to me and said, "Not so fast, Doc. Take a hit. It's the good shit." I said, "I wouldn't know." Then I rubbed out the cherry and handed it to Jerry. "Hang on to that," I said. "Evidence." On the hospital roof that night, Jerry and I conducted an examination. Based on the evidence, we concluded we were higher than every tree in town.

Selective Amnesia

We were sitting in a Cadillac in the driveway, watching our house burn. The flames lit up the neighborhood like an angry confession lights up a bedroom. You said, "Remember how you used to scare me?" I said, "Yes. No. Wait—I used to scare you? In what way?" You didn't answer, and as our house belly-flopped and hissed into the neighbor's pool, I wondered what else I'd been keeping from myself.

TWO SHOTS

Over the dunes came dune buggies with makeshift machine-gun mounts. I could barely make out the faces of the mutants, but man, did they look pissed. We ducked beneath the boardwalk beneath the charred sky and tried to formulate a plan. I asked whether you could run. You frowned and slapped the sides of your wheelchair. You said, "Nope. Still real. Still really in a wheelchair." I bit my thumb lightly, then, enjoying the pain, bit a little harder. Then I bit it right off and spat it onto your lap. I said, "Fuck! Well you can dig, can't you?" But it was too late. The mutants were nearly upon us lepers. I said, "It's time I told you my secret." You said, "You can fly?" I said, "No, I'm a coward." Then I pulled my gun and shot me first.

Happy America, America!

A room-service cart filled with bacon and eggs and pancakes. That was the order, but I slept through breakfast. By afternoon, you were across the country, in Memphis, making out with a busboy on a busted porch outside an Elvis motel. I ordered more room service: a couple Heinekens, a Bloody Mary, and a birthday cake with my name on it. It was the 4th of July. I dialed up a pay-per-view porno. Freedom meant something different to each of us. And that's what made America America. *Viva Las Vegas*, I sang to myself as I rubbed one out—and it felt so patriotic and good! I went over to the window and swiped my cum on it. I gazed down at the strip. Yes, I felt like some middle-class version of Howard Hughes. I was a man without a plan—hung over and already half-drunk—and just stupid enough to think everything was going to be all right.

Measured and True

It all came down to this, this one moment where one of us would prove to be the champion and the other would prove to be the first loser. Inside the coliseum we circled each other until our circle swallowed itself, leaving us toe to toe. The crowd was noisy and bloated, begging for blood. I reared back and aimed for your nose. You bent low and aimed an uppercut at my heart. Your blow was measured and true. I was a celebrity addict who couldn't change the channel, and now I see stars forever.

My Mother Was a Virgin: A Posthumous Memoir

My mother was a virgin. One day she poured wine into her wine glass. I closed my eyes, muttered some mumbo-jumbo, and turned the wine into water. She took a sip, and I snapped my fingers and set the water on fire. She spat fire, said, "Look. This has got to stop. Go practice your goddamn 'miracles' outside." And so I went outside and then I went outside outside—I went outside the world and stayed out there until I died alone on a lonely planet.

XIII.

In the wilds of AstroTurf Park.

Behind the Non-Denominational Fitness Center.

I looked both ways before crossing my fingers.

Like the fourth man on the Moon,

I, too, have felt like giving up.

Runaway Rex, Part Deux

We took a drive to the country for something to do, but once we passed the county line, you said you didn't understand what you saw anymore, that the country looked like another country altogether. I said, "Buckle up," because I saw the same thing, too. We passed a two-headed crow in a palm tree, and then the doors sucked out and the roof curled back. Through a winter wind, all around came a strange anthem from the radio. At first it sounded like heaven. Then it sounded like hell. We squeezed our muskets and squinted through the bug-spattered windshield at the war ahead. The fight would grow ugly. You'd lose your mother. I'd lose my virginity to your sister. She'd lose our first child, but we'd have another, a girl this time with a vestigial tail and one good angel wing. Cancer would take most of us in the end, though you'd die from a malignant tumor behind your eyes. But oh, the sights you'd see! From your hospital bed, you'd recite things like cranberry lake, toxic moon, jacked Buddy Hackett. "Dude is big!" you'd say. I'd squeeze your hand, and you'd squeeze your morphine drip. Then I thought, 'Shit!' because you weren't even gone yet, but I missed you already. That's when I noticed the dog keeping pace alongside the car. I hadn't seen him since I was a boy. I pulled over as gently as I could. I didn't want to miss this reunion.

THE CAST

Mel Bosworth is the author of the novel, *Freight*, and the poetry chapbook, *Every Laundromat in the World*. He lives in Western Massachusetts.

Ryan Ridge is the author of three books, including *American Homes* (University of Michigan Press, 2015), which was the Michigan Library Publishing Club's inaugural book club pick. His writing has appeared in dozens of print and online journals, as well as several anthologies. In 2016, Ridge received the Italo Calvino Prize in Fabulist Fiction, judged by Jonathan Lethem. An assistant professor at Weber State University, he lives in Salt Lake City and edits the literary magazine, *Juked*.

Jacob Heustis is an artist living in Louisville, Kentucky. Since 2004, he has exhibited at Swanson Contemporary, the Green Building Gallery, Land of

Tomorrow, Zephyr Gallery, Actor's Theatre, Kentucky School of Art, Brown Theatre, Hite Art Institute, The Speed Art Museum, Cressman Center for Visual Arts, Kentucky Museum of Art and Craft, and 21C Bentonville, Durham, and Cincinnati. Recent work has appeared in *New American Paintings*.

Acknowledgments

Huge thanks to the editors of the journals in which these pieces previously appeared, sometimes in slightly different forms or under slightly different titles.

Periodicals

Big Lucks: "Blue Christmas," "E = Nude∞," "Group Therapy," "It's Not Easy Being Green Cheese," "Littlest Big Man," "Songs for a Better Life"

the EEEL: "American Adventure," "A New Kind of Hump Day," "Cowboy Candy," "Everything That Was Ever Wrong," "Fair's Fair," "Fireworks," "Immortality Sucks," "Keys," "Magic Hour," "My Head My Voice My Shoes My Toes," "Sanctuary"

Fanzine: "Another Us," "A Spike in Teen Pregnancy"

Faultline: "Light Eaters," "Maggie," "The Opposite of Forgettable," "Our Old Skins," "Search Party," "Two Shots"

The Greenbelt Review: "IX."

Hobart: "A Percentage of Those Who Wander Are Lost," "Encore," "The Fattest Man in the Smallest Seat," "The Gospel of Puke," "Inquire Within," "Johnny Depp Prepares for His Role as Raoul Duke," "Let's Make a Deal (Family Edition)," "Life," "Missing Children," "The Pretender," "Recovery," "True Story"

Kitty Snacks: "I.," "III.," "V.," "VII.," "XI."

McSweeney's Small Chair: "The Biggest Hearts in the World Cannot Be Tethered," "Bottom Blood," "Escape to No Escape," "I Said What I Said," "Little Buddy," "Midnight Safari," "The Next Hieroglyph," "The Poet Addresses a Proud Nation," "Salad Days," "Summer Somewhere," "Swapping Spit," "Where the Doors Went"

MonkeyBicycle: "Best Western"

NERVE: "Afterlife Insurance," "Beat Too Long," "I Read the News Today," "No Retreat," "Slick MF," "Temp-to-Fire Agency"

Passages North: "All Talk and No Follow-Through," "Hot Date with History," "Istanbul," "Last Decade," "The Lollipop Guild Breaks

Bad," "Vanishing Act"

Salt Hill: "XIII."

Santa Monica Review: "Cuckolding down the Fort," "The Events as They Unfolded," "Everything's True Intention," "Our Flag Was Still There," "Happy America, America!" "The House Always Wins," "How We Came to Live ...," "Lost Scenes from the Little League World Series Parking Lot," "Measured and True," "Memphis Blood," "My Mother Was a Virgin ...," "The Time I Got into a Knife Fight but Forgot My Knife," "Tomorrow, We'll Be Rested," "Separated at Birth," "Ultimate Ultimatum," "Your Life and Nearly Mine," "Tuxedo Dogs"

Sleepingfish: "Beginner's Luck," "I Can See Paradise," "It's Alright, Ma (I'm Only Burning)," "The Only Way out Is In," "Opposite Day," "Our Finest Crime," "Our Own Little Private Party," "Return Flight," "Sans Sensei," "Somewhere in the Starburst," "The Son Will Burn You, Eventually"

Sundog Lit: "APParition," "Elvis Costello Has Left the Building," "Ground Rules," "Pickup Artists," "Runaway Rex," "Vacation from Vacation"

Tin House: "A String of Hot Seconds," "Exaltation," "No One Can Hear the Cotton Screams of Ronnie James Dio," "Our Tolerance of Youth," "Sitcom Stars Storm the Beach"

Unmanned Press: "An Introduction to Gender and Sexuality," "Different Jurisdictions," "Donner Party Time," "Go Wildcats!" "Honolulu of the Heart," "Heartbreak Special"

ANTHOLOGIES

They Said: A Multi-Genre Anthology of Contemporary Collaborative Writing (Black Lawrence Press), "from Second Acts."

NOTES

"II.," "IV.," "VI.," "VIII.," "X.," and "XII." appeared in *Every Laundromat in the World*, a limited-edition chapbook by Safety Third Enterprises.

"Where the Doors Went" was a finalist for *Best Small Fictions 2016* (Stuart Dybek, editor).

Colophon

What you are holding is the First Edition of this short-story collection in this current form. A partial edition was previously published under a different title from a now-defunct press.

The alternating title fonts are Alpaca54 by Dirt2, Acidic by Surface Type, and Porcelain by Misprinted Type. The back cover Alternating Current Press font is Portmanteau by JLH Fonts. All other type is set in Calisto MT.

Cover artwork is created, modified, and designed by Leah Angstman and Michael Litos, with artwork by Anja at coco-parisienne. Interior illustrations are by Jacob Heustis, ©2018.

The lightbulb logo was created by Leah Angstman, ©2006, 2018 Alternating Current. Mel Bosworth's photo was taken by Christy Crutchfield, ©2017, 2018. Ryan Ridge's photo was taken by Sarah Lyon, ©2017, 2018. Jacob Heustis' photo was taken by Elizabeth Kramer, ©2017, 2018.

All fonts, artwork, graphics, and designs were used with permission. All rights reserved. The publisher wishes to thank all artwork, graphic, and font creators for their generosity in allowing legal use.

alternatingcurrentarts.com

Made in the USA
Columbia, SC
12 February 2018